CYNDY SZEKERE

Favorite
Mother
Goose
Rhymes

Selected and illustrated by
Cyndy Szekeres

A GOLDEN BOOK • NEW YORK

Western Publishing Company, Inc., Racine, Wisconsin 53404

Cackle, Cackle, Mother Goose

Cackle, cackle, Mother Goose,
Have you any feathers loose?
Truly have I, pretty fellow,
Half enough to fill a pillow.
Here are quills, take one or two,
And down to make a bed for you.

4

Cock Crows In The Morn

Cock crows in the morn
    To tell us to rise,
And he who lies late
    Will never be wise;
For early to bed
    And early to rise,
Is the way to be healthy
    And wealthy and wise.

Cock-A-Doodle-Doo!

Cock-a-doodle-doo!
My dame has lost her shoe;
My master's lost his fiddlestick
And knows not what to do.

5

Pat-A-Cake, Pat-A-Cake

Pat-a-cake, pat-a-cake,
     Baker's man,
Bake me a cake
     As fast as you can.
Pat it, and prick it,
     And mark it with B,
And put it in the oven
     For Baby and me.

Hot-Cross Buns

Hot-cross buns!
Hot-cross buns!
One a penny, two a penny,
Hot-cross buns!

If your daughters do not like them,
Give them to your sons.
One a penny, two a penny,
Hot-cross buns!

6

Pease Porridge Hot

Pease porridge hot,
Pease porridge cold,
Pease porridge in the pot
Nine days old.
Some like it hot,
Some like it cold,
Some like it in the pot
Nine days old.

Hush, Baby, My Dolly

Hush, baby, my dolly,
    I pray you don't cry,
And I'll give you some bread,
    And some milk by and by;
Or perhaps you like custard,
    Or maybe a tart?
Then to either you're welcome,
    With all of my heart.

Old Mother Hubbard

Old Mother Hubbard went to the cupboard
To fetch her poor dog a bone;
But when she got there, the cupboard was bare,
And so her poor dog had none.

Little Miss Muffet

Little Miss Muffet
Sat on a tuffet,
Eating her curds and whey;
When along came a spider,
Who sat down beside her,
And frightened Miss Muffet away.

Little Tom Tucker

Little Tom Tucker
Sings for his supper.
What shall he eat?
White bread and butter.
How will he cut it
Without any knife?
How will he marry
Without any wife?

Little Jack Horner

Little Jack Horner
Sat in a corner,
Eating a Christmas pie;
He put in his thumb,
And pulled out a plum,
And said, "What a good boy am I!"

Hey Diddle Diddle

Hey diddle diddle,
    The cat and the fiddle,
The cow jumped over the moon.
    The little dog laughed
    To see such sport,
And the dish ran away with the spoon.

10

There Was an Old Woman Tossed In A Blanket

There was an old woman tossed in a blanket
Seventeen times as high as the moon;
But where she was going no mortal could tell,
For under her arm she carried a broom.
"Old woman, old woman, old woman," said I,
"Whither, ah whither, ah whither so high?"
"To sweep the cobwebs from the sky,
And I'll be with you by and by."

11

Little Bo-Peep

Little Bo-Peep has lost her sheep
And can't tell where to find them;
Leave them alone and they'll come home,
Wagging their tails behind them.

Baa, Baa, Black Sheep

Baa, baa, black sheep,
Have you any wool?
Yes, sir, yes, sir,
Three bags full;

One for my master,
And one for my dame,
And one for the little boy
Who lives down the lane.

Mary Had A Little Lamb

Mary had a little lamb,
Its fleece was white as snow;
And everywhere that Mary went
The lamb was sure to go.

It followed her to school one day,
Which was against the rule;
It made the children laugh and play
To see a lamb at school.

And so the teacher turned it out,
But still it lingered near,
And waited patiently about
Till Mary did appear.

"Why does the lamb love Mary so?"
The eager children cry.
"Why, Mary loves the lamb, you know,"
The teacher did reply.

There Was An Old Woman Who Lived In A Shoe

There was an old woman
　　　Who lived in a shoe,
She had so many children,
　　　She didn't know what to do.
So she gave them some broth
　　　Without any bread,
And hugged them and kissed them
　　　And put them to bed.

14

Little Jumping Joan

Here am I, little jumping Joan,
When nobody's with me
I'm always alone.

15

1, 2, Buckle My Shoe

1, 2, buckle my shoe;
3, 4, shut the door;
5, 6, pick up sticks;
7, 8, lay them straight;
9, 10, a good fat hen;
11, 12, I hope you're well;
13, 14, draw the curtain;

15, 16, maid in the kitchen;
17, 18, there she's waiting;
19, 20, my stomach's empty.

Rub-A-Dub-Dub, Three Men In A Tub

Rub-a-dub-dub, three men in a tub,
    And who do you think they be?
The butcher, the baker, the candlestick-maker,
    And all of them going to sea.

Peter Piper

Peter Piper picked a peck of pickled peppers;
A peck of pickled peppers did Peter Piper pick.
If Peter Piper picked a peck of pickled peppers,
Where are the peppers that Peter Piper picked?

Rain, Rain, Go Away

Rain, rain, go away,
Come again another day,
Little Johnny wants to play.

18

Peter, Peter, Pumpkin Eater

Peter, Peter, pumpkin eater,
Had a wife and couldn't keep her;
He put her in a pumpkin shell,
And there he kept her very well.

Handy-Spandy, Jack-A-Dandy

Handy-spandy, Jack-a-dandy,
Loves plum cake and sugar candy.
He bought some at a grocer's shop,
And, pleased, away went hop, hop, hop.

Jack, Be Nimble

Jack, be nimble, Jack, be quick;
Jack, jump over the candlestick.

Diddle Diddle Dumpling

Diddle diddle dumpling, my son John
Went to bed with his trousers on;
One shoe off and one shoe on,
Diddle diddle dumpling, my son John.

21

Wee Willie Winkie

Wee Willie Winkie
    Runs through the town,
Upstairs and downstairs,
    In his nightgown;
Tapping at the window,
    Crying at the lock;
"Are all the children in their beds,
    For now it's eight o'clock?"